FLASHLIGHT NIGHT

Matt Forrest Esenwine
Illustrated by Fred Koehler

BOYDS MILLS PRESS
AN IMPRINT OF HIGHLIGHTS
Honesdale, Pennsylvania

To Phoebe, Grey, Katie, Lauren, and Jess, who inspire me every day.
—MFE

To the adventurers: this book is for you.
—FK

The illustrator offers special thanks to: Matt for captivating my imagination; Rebecca Davis for pushing and Tracey Adams for pulling; Abby and Jack for the scathing, real-time critique; the Southward family for lending me AJ; Jane Yolen, Heidi Stemple, and Debby Harris for tying the tea towel at Wayside; Hazel Mitchell for the inside information; Laura Bowers for the Turkish Delight and Sarah for sharing it with me; and the helpful staff members who assisted with research at the following places: Manchester Museum, The John Rylands Library, The Mary Rose Museum, YHA Ambleside, YHA Lulworth Cove, St. Giles Cathedral, Wray Castle, and Greyfriars Kirkyard.

BOYDS MILLS PRESS
An Imprint of Highlights
815 Church Street
Honesdale, Pennsylvania 18431
Printed in China

ISBN: 978-1-62979-493-8
Library of Congress Control Number: 2016959861

First edition
The text of this book is set in Garamond Premier.
The illustrations were created in pencil and colored digitally.

10 9 8 7 6 5 4 3 2 1

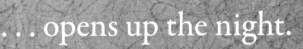

. . . opens up the night.

Leads you past old post and rail
along a long-forgotten trail

into woods no others dare,
for fear of what is waiting there.

Shines a path where waters rush,
reveals a hole in the underbrush.

Casts a glow upon a wall
down a dark and ancient hall

as inky shadows rise and fall,
dancing . . .

to no sound at all.

Deep inside a narrow room,
unmasks a time-forgotten tomb

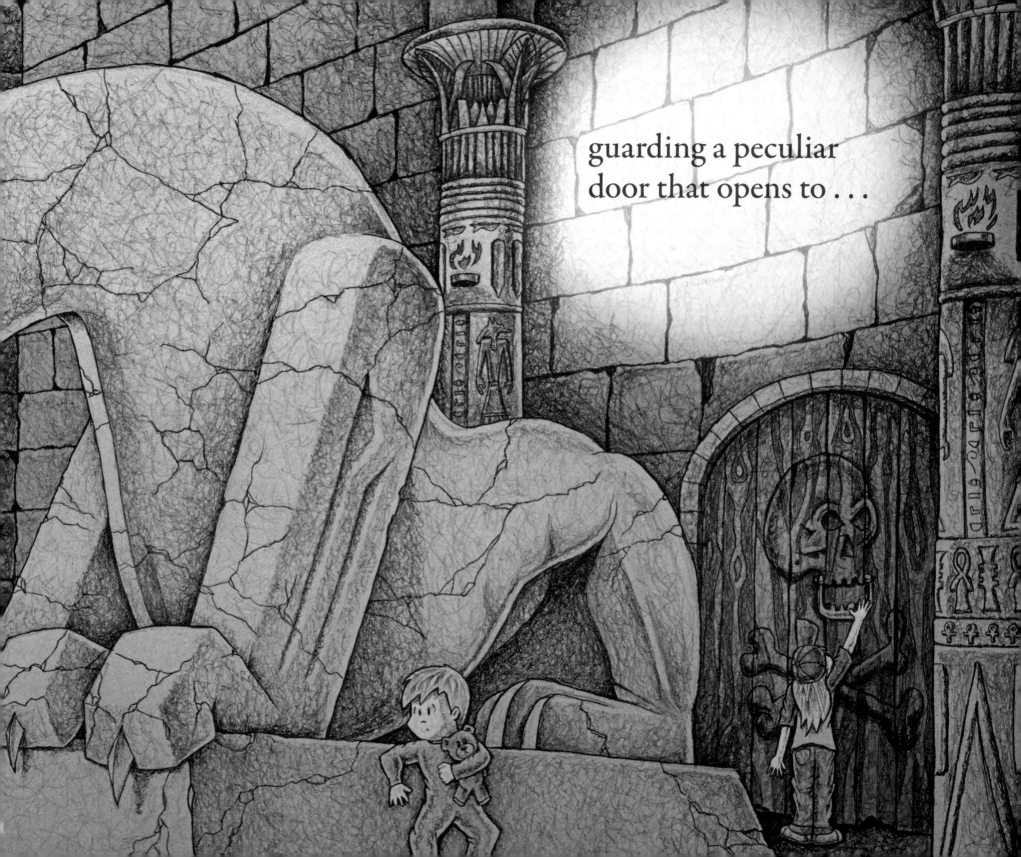

...a foreign shore.

Finds a vessel, tightly moored,
helps you slyly sneak aboard.

Brightens deck and mizzenmast,
exposes what you're sailing past.

Shows a stealthy way to flee—
across cool sand, around a tree,

up a craggy mountainside—

through a window, open wide,

sinking under covers deep
as weary eyes fight off the sleep.

Adventure lingers,
stirs about—

until a voice says,

"*Shhh . . .*